To Lupita,

Your loving spirit shines down upon us always.

For information regarding permission, please write to:

Maya & Me Publications
12060 County Line Rd., Suite J #197
Madison, AL 35756
www.maya-and-me.com

ISBN: 978-0-692-47111-1

Printed in the United States of America

Hi, my name is Maya, and this is a story about my Daddy.

He takes care of me every day.

He is making blueberry waffles, and they smell so good.

Daddy's day is off to a busy start.

Breakfast is ready.
I look down at my
waffle and giggle.

Daddy made a happy
face with blueberries.

While I finish my breakfast, Daddy packs my lunch bag with all my favorite healthy foods.

He always makes sure I eat my fruits and veggies.

What will I wear today? We choose the perfect outfit.

He helps me double-knot my sneakers.

My hair is still messy, but we don't have much time.

Daddy gives me a quick, simple style that will last all day.

It's off to school.

Daddy packs all my
books and supplies
in my book bag.

While I'm in class, Daddy is working hard at home,

cleaning and organizing.

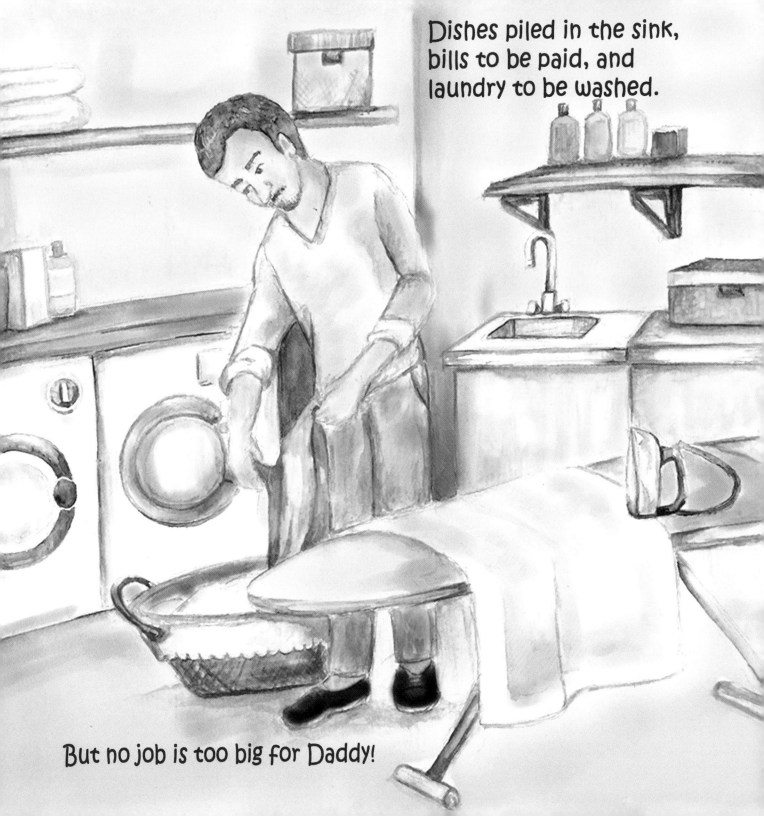

School is done for the day. It's time for Daddy to pick me up.

He's waiting in the car line.

Here I come!
He greets me with
a wink and a smile.
Lets hit the road.

It's Wednesday afternoon, and my gymnastics class will begin soon.

Today we practice tumbling.

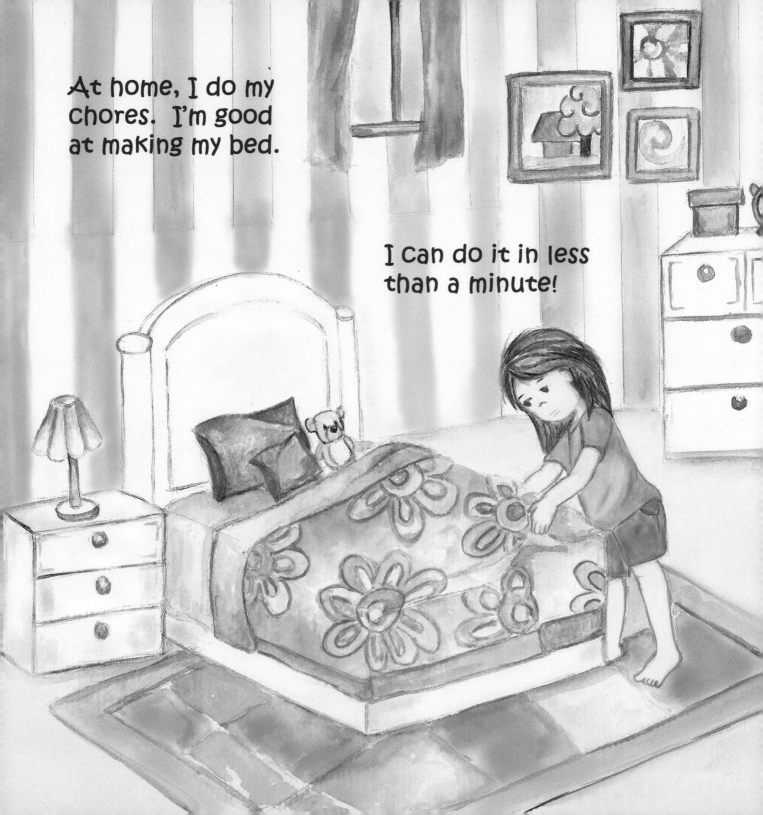

Daddy says I can play with our
dog before dinner. He joins me.
It's so fun when Daddy plays with us.

Afterward, Daddy pulls out my
homework from my school folder.
We look it over together.

He says, "Great effort, Maya"
when I finish my assignment.

Daddy starts making dinner.
It's my choice tonight.

Tomato soup and grilled cheese sandwiches!

Just then, I hear the front door open. Mommy's home!

Daddy and I give her a kiss and he takes her bag.

I sit on the couch with Mommy.

She asks about my day while
Daddy finishes making dinner.

Mommy loves the pictures I drew in class. I tell
her about the story the teacher read to us.

Daddy calls us for dinner. The soup looks yummy.

I can't wait to sip the first spoonful. We say a prayer. Now, it's time to eat.

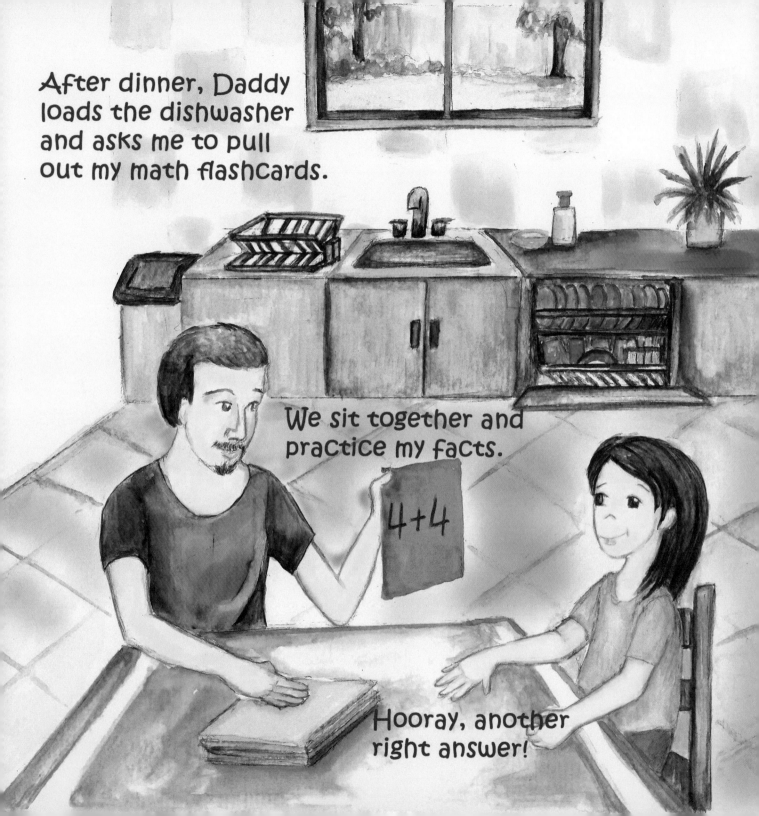

While Mommy works on her laptop, Daddy reminds me that martial arts class is tomorrow.

I will earn my next color belt if I pass my test.

Daddy helps me practice the moves. He takes martial arts, too.

He knows a lot about turns and sidekicks. He won a trophy once!

It's almost bedtime.
Time to take a bath.
Daddy adds some
bubbles.

I have all my toys ready.

Mommy picks out some pajamas, while I finish my bath.

I sing my favorite songs in the tub.

Mommy helps me dress
and dries my hair.

Daddy reminds
me to brush
and floss my
teeth.

I choose my bedtime story for Daddy to read.

It's a book about patience.

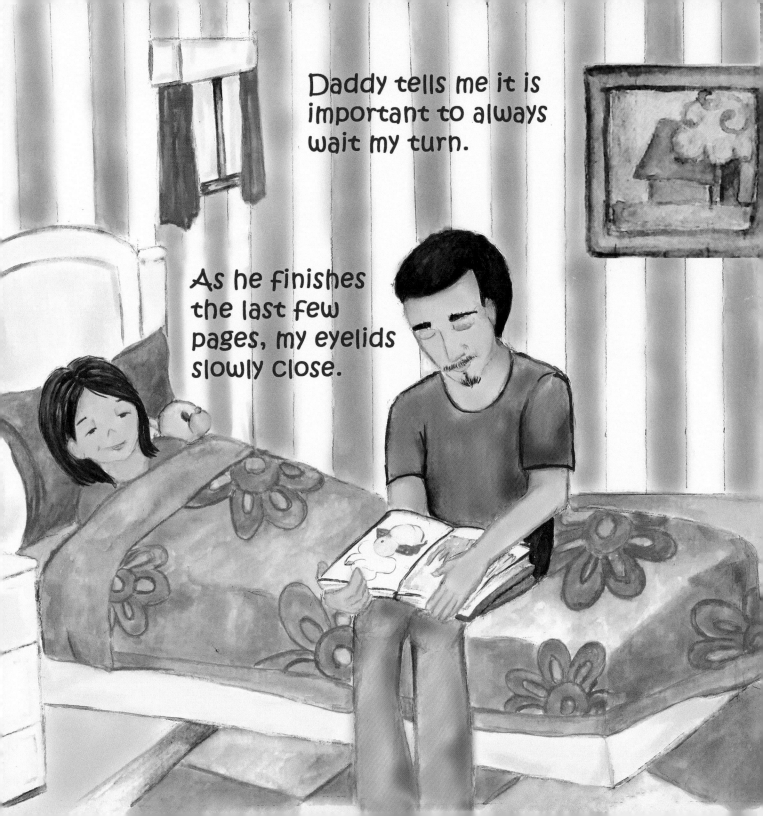

Daddy tells me it is important to always wait my turn.

As he finishes the last few pages, my eyelids slowly close.

It has been another action-packed day with Daddy. Now, onto new adventures!

CPSIA information can be obtained at www.ICGtesting.com
Printed in the USA
BVIW12n0135141216
470751BV00016B/89